Bushveld
Diary in Africa

Bushveld Diary in Africa

Hitch Hiker

iUniverse, Inc.
Bloomington

Bushveld Diary in Africa

iUniverse books may be ordered through booksellers or by contacting:

iUniverse
1663 Liberty Drive
Bloomington, IN 47403
www.iuniverse.com
1-800-Authors (1-800-288-4677)

ISBN: 978-1-4620-3442-0 (pbk)
ISBN: 978-1-4620-3443-7 (ebk)

Printed in the United States of America

iUniverse rev. date: 07/11/2011

THIS BOOK IS DEDICATED TO

people in need, with the hope that as long as there is finances coming in from my books as a writer to invest in those that are willing to go forward in peace, and hopefully reach as much as possible hiv/aids patients worldwide foodwise.

ABOUT THE AUTHOR

A practicle person with an ambition to see people in a happier position, a person that traveled some parts of the world mostly on his furniture money to reach his gaols in life.

We can serve a God, but if we don't do the practical in a good balance with the theoratical side, our scales will always hang off balance, and it's normaly people and mostly children that will suffer because of it.

We must feed people, before we start to learn people.

What ever happens in your life, keep holding on to your vision (goals) in life?

"BUSHVELD DIARY IN AFRICA"

Early in the morning, 5.30 am.

Today will be an extreme hot day; I can feel the heat already on my skin. As I look towards the bushveld horizon, it's as if the thorn trees are in place to prevent the son from coming up from the east, as if they know they will be part of this heat period that awaits us all today.

I took my rifle hanged it over my right shoulder and choose my direction towards the bush. My eye catches my strawberry land on my left side, maybe there will be an intruder looking for something to fill his stomach with, nothing this morning. I met John, one off the farm workers on my way; he will always follow me when he sees a rifle hanging on my shoulder. The other workers must start to clean the wheat in between the strawberry lanes. I have learned some off John's ways in the bush, he knows the direction off a spoor (track). He can tell which direction we must go, once we found a spoor, he will keep a track like a blood hound.

In the bush you need sharp trained eyes and ears.

I found John an African on another farm, staying all by himself with his wife and children, getting not much to live on, if you look at his skinny condition at age of a fourty year old man, you can see the unbalanced life he lived. Not a man of many words, but always on your side, a very practical person, one reason we can work together. I can leave John on the farm and go to the city to deliver jam's, and know that there will be a good eye on the farm. He will take a pair of pliers and wire and fix what's wrong on the farm. You need someone like John as your right hand, he will back you with his life in emergency situations, whatever happens, and he will be there to assist you in the bush or on the farm 24 hours.

This morning I stood up and thought of getting meat for the farm workers, but off cause to enjoy the hunt too. As soon as we enter the thorn bush area, we kept quiet for hunting reasons, eyes on any movement and ears tuned in for the rite sounds. We are in this bush today to get a warthog, (kind off pick) because farm workers like any meat they can get. (I believe the one reason Africa is dying in such totals off HIV/AIDS is the unbalanced diet they take in daily, the amount of maize they take in without any vegetables.)

To be part of the African bush is a good feeling, but don't let it catch you off-side. Same with the African people, most off the time they will fall back on their African roots. Roots we as the western world most of the time doesn't understand, a way we struggle to understand in Africa, if the different cultures give each other enough room, we will be able to live together in Africa in a much better way of understanding. **Question: how can one culture rule over another culture?**

Early In the morning, the chances are normally good to find any kind of animal to hunt. Today we must find meat for the farm workers, and it feels good to come home with meat. John touches my shoulder with his hand; this is one of the ways we communicate in the bush. He saw something, and immediately my eye catches his reason for touching me on the shoulder, warthog about fourty meters in front of us. All my concentration kicks in.

Two adult warthogs are close to the waterhole, and we are on the right side of the wind so that they can't smell us, if we were upwind they would've smelt us. This is the way I like it, on our feet and on their level. When you see a warthog, you will have 5-8 seconds to pull the trigger, a bird can warn them with one whistle. A warthog can smell you from a long distance, if you don't keep on checking on the wind direction, you can walk for the whole day, and come back home with only tired feet and empty pick-up.

I lift my .303 rifle very slowly, today it's very easy, they still don't know about us. I look through the telescope and picked the bigger one of the two, the bore. I put the telescope cross right on the centre of it shoulder, just behind the neck. John stands like a dead tree just behind me with his eyes on the warthog, ready to run, like a 100 meter athlete waiting for the gunshot to go off. I pull the trigger slowly towards me, you only need to move your trigger finger, if you pull with your whole hand you will move the rifle of the target and misses completely; I can feel the concentration around me and the sweat in the palm of my hand. As soon as the shot goes the pig drops dead in its last position, the other one ran away on high speed, and so did John towards the kicking pig, his shiny yes and smile shows his happiness. He knows that I barely misses a pig, because I learned to hunt on them.

We pulled the warthog under one off the trees for shade, and make our way back to the house to get the Isussu pickup. To hunt in the African bush is easy if you know the bush, or with someone that learn by growing up here.

When you hunt you work together, you can only work together if you listen to the one that knows the bush.

I parked the pickup next to the tree where we left the pig, and open the tailgate to make it easier for us to swing the pig up onto the back of the pickup. John will always sit on the back of the bakkie after a hunt, this is how the farmers trained them in the early days, and they are still doing it. Most times they are the eyes for the hunters. You can scan the bush much better with your eyes when you stand on the back of the pickup, kudu level. With a soft knock on the caps roof, the driver will know you have seen something. He will apply the brakes as slowly as he can, as soon as the pickup stops, he will switch the vehicle of to give the hunter a change to take aim without vehicle vibration. (pickup hunt, is most of the time for people that can't walk in the bush)

I can still see the happiness on John's face as I look in my rear mirror. MEAT TONIGHT!!!
The fire will burn very high tonight, and the talking will be much later than other nights.

Maybe there is something you as the reader can pick up in these people's lives. They are waiting every day for something to happen to bring them on a high for only that specific day, something positive to live for.

Tomorrow, hopefully there will be something new to uplift them to carry on, something to discuss around the fire tonight. It is sad just to be a number, a voting number. (X)

After 10 am we're back in the strawberry land joining the other workers, and you can hear the conversation between the workers as John transfer the whole hunting story in detail, while they busy checking the water for the strawberries.

I know they can't wait for 5 o'clock, to go home to start the fire. Today they will gather more wood as usual.

The day end on a happy note, and even I feel good on their behalf.

IT'S GOOD TO SEE PEOPLE HAPPY!!!

My name is Johan van der Schyff, born on the 11/12/1959 in Pretoria, South Africa.

Dumped on an early age into an orphanage, I struggled through life with no self confidence, but always tried to make the right decisions with a pure heart, not always accurate, but pure.

One of my biggest heart desires will always be to ask a father if my decision is right or wrong, you know, just to discuss certain things with him to make sure I'm on the right track. Some of you will know what I'm talking about.

(Read my book called
    "THE HITCH HIKER/TEXAS")

I have spend some of my life as a strawberry and gooseberry farmer in a area called Vivo in the Northern part of Southern Africa, where you will find one off the world's most undiscovered mountain strips in the world, the Soutpansberg mountains. The name came from the saltpans at the foot of the mountain on the northern side of the mountain. You will also find extreme heat up to 50 degrees at time in this area, and if you don't protect yourself against this extreme nature, it will sort you out in a way you would not like. You must handle the bushveld like a marathon, don't start on high speed. Keep a decent pace and top yourself up with water as you go through the day. Cover yourself. (HAT)

You can't change this area, it will kill you. Learn it ways, and you will survive. When you hunt, you can move from tree to tree to get some shade over you, and never leave your house without your hat, and make sure it's a hat with good ventilation.

You will always be an outsider if you're not born here. People don't trust each other, they will be your friend today, and tomorrow they will stab you in the back with their stories against you. You are never at ease with them.

I went to the bushveld because I longed for that since my childhood, and it's a dream that came true in my life. I suffered in the bushveld because of the heat, give me ice and I'm happy, but I enjoyed it like no one else. I farmed on a piece of land I rent from a rich farmer that you can never make your friend.

And then the hunting, free to take your rifle and walk into the bush, to be yourself, learning the birds, the tree's, the insects, the animals, and the sounds of the bush. What a life with no boarders.

You can hunt any kind of animal you want, with a price off cause, and the farmers know how to ad a price to any animal you want to hunt, believe me. Don't be mistaken it's worth it; it's an experience you will remember for the rest of your life.

Most of the farmers are potato farmers, and then of cause hunting, where they make some of their money in the winter times.

My first hunting trip started on another farmer's farm where he tried to farm with maize. John was there right on my side. Once you plant maize in the bushveld you will soon realize you are the centre point for all warthogs in the bushveld. Warthogs will come many kilometers for maize and stay in the land for weeks. The maize supply is the food, and the water sickle the water, what better place for a warthog to stay for weeks.

Anybody that wants to hunt warthogs can sit next to the maize lands and wait for these fully packed maize pigs to appear in the open. You can hear them coming, because of the noise the leaves are making. It's not really a hunt, but for me for sure.

I parked my Issusu pickup about 500 meters from the maize land and we walked in a forward bend position towards a thorn tree to cover our selfs with the shade. We must get our selfs in a position so that we can see left and right. You don't have any idea witch side they going to come out of the maize land. We must be ready; you can never put nature in a box. Nature will come to you in a way you expect the least.

I can feel the adrenalin pumping, and the sweat on the palms of my hands tells me that I'm nervous. I relaxed my whole body to calm down, but keep my finger on the trigger, just in case my first pig arrives. Remember it's my first hunt and it's on a warthog. I can see John in the corner of my right eye, no sound or move from him, only his eyes are moving left and right, he knows every movement can cost us a warthog, and that means no meat for them as well.

We waited, and waited, 15 min. 30 min, and then we hear the bottom maize leaves are cracking as it slides on the side of the pig's body. One good thing of a warthog is that when it gets outside the maize land or through a fence, it will stand still in the open for +- five to eight seconds, just enough time for you to lift your rifle; put the cross on the spot, and to pull the trigger.

Well this one was coming straight towards us, and I decided to shoot him while his still about 5 meters in the maize land. I lifted my rifle in the direction of the rumbling leaves, telescope cross on the pig and pulled the trigger; I shot the pig right from the front. The pig dropped on the spot, everything around us stopped, no sound off birds no rumbling maize leaves, no moving pig, and then the bird sound came back, and nature carries on like nothing happens.

I reloaded immediately, just in case the pig decided to stand up and run, or other pigs run out of the land. You never know if they are more than one. The teeth of a warthog can rip you open and kill you instantly. The body of a worthhog are a solid ball of muscle, and you don't want to be in the way of those two white swords sticking out on either side of that mouth.

I got out of the shade and walk slowly towards the spot where I know the pig must lie, John is waiting in the shade, rifle ready for anything that wants to move, I will put another bullet rite through it. As I get to the beginning of the maize land, the pig jumped up and came straight at me, just misses my left leg, I turned around, without lifting the rifle, I just pulled the trigger with the rifle in the pigs direction, I hit it in the stomach, the pig rolled over, once or twice, before it lies still for good. Nature's quiet again.

From that day on, I got trained by hunting warthogs, if you can shoot a warthog in the run, you will be able to hunt many other animals in the bush.

I shot my biggest warthog next to this maize land; tell you the story later, with a photo;

What makes the African bush so special? The fact that it infects your life daily and you're not aware of it, till you go away for a month. Then the thorn, baobab, njala tree and bush sound with no stretched out birds, and the mountain will call you back.

Every day in the bushveld will be a suffering. You don't just live here, you suffer to live here. The heat's so extreme that you can bake eggs on a rock in ten minutes. You can't walk without shoes or slops, day and night. In the day against heat and snakes, and at night against snakes and scorpions you can't see.

Never ever walk at night without a light, the chances are good that you will get bitten or stung by something you not aware of.

You must turn your boots around and bang it against the floor before you put it on your feet. Scorpions like to get into boots for cover. Never put your hand inside a schoe or a boot, you will go to hospital, when a black thick tale scorpion gets hold of you. They reckon its poison is equal than the poison of a black mamba snake, scary snake, the mamba.

Never pickup sticks or small tree branches, unless you are sure it's not a snake. The mamba can climb a tree by standing up rite 2 thirds of its body to reach the lower tree branches to get into a tree.

One big problem snake will always be the puff adder, short, thick fat snake. One of the fastest striking snakes you can get, you will not be able to see its strike. You will just feel a pain in the bottom part of your leg, then you must make for the hospital, otherwise you will lose your leg, or maybe a hand. The doctors give you 25 minutes to safe your limb, after that, sorry. Best way not to get bitten, stay with the rule, remember what you have learned from those who know.

I had a case where my neighbour visited me with his stuffy dog, a beautiful light brown dog, real Jock of the bushveld size dog. Rite outside my gate the dog went for something in the grass that I have cut down with the bush cutter about two days earlier. The dog was running around his owner already bitten rite in the neck. The owner didn't see the strike of the snake, so he wasn't sure if the dog were bitten or not.

He called me, and I brought my knob kierie (cane) along. I found the snake, puff adder, still lying on the spot, ready for the next strike; I hit the puff adder right on the head with the first strike that killed the snake instantly. I picked the puff adder up, at least one meter long and thick like my fore-arm, 10cm in diameter.

At this stage we could see that the dog got bitten. We grapped the dog put it into the vehicle and drove for town, we phoned the vet on the way, and he waited for us, as we put the dog onto his stainless steel table, the dog died.

The puff adder bit him rite in the neck, he suffocates on his way to the vet. Seventy five kilometers were too far. The dog was like a child to the old man.

If you get bitten by a mamba in the bush, you must make sure you have greeted everybody; it's a lot of poison a snake can pump into you in a split second. I got stung by a scorpion in the palm of my hand once. Luckily it was a thin tale, and I survived it. It's like a thousand needles that keep on jumping up and down for a day or two around the bitten area.

When you are a new visitor in the bushveld, listen to the people that know the bush. Remember the things you have learned from them. Then you will survive. I don't like snakes, if they get to my house. I sort them out. If there's a rat somewhere around your living area, you will find mamba and puff adder at least.

Snakes are doing wonderfull work in nature, never try to copy the people on television and think it's easy to handle snakes, snakes are fast, and they can spit very accurately. Not many snakes are poisonous. You must know snakes; we can't kill all snakes, because nature needs them.

If you do come across a snake, move away very slowly in a different direction if possible.

"IT'S GOOD TO LEARN ABOUT NATURE"

"Bird on leadwood"

Every morning when the farm workers arrive on the farm, two of them will walk around the home fence to look for snake sailing spoors.

What's very important is that we must clean our fences from any growing nature. At least two meters on both sides of the fence, firstly for preventing fires to come close to your land and house, and then for entering snakes into your living space. If they do find that a snake entered your living area, they look for the exit marks as well, if they don't find any exit marks, we must look till we find the snake. We normally know if it's big or not.

In the mornings the workers pick up all the tree branches that fell from trees during the previous night. If you see small branches on the short cut lawn, you must make sure it's not a snake on its way to your house.

Johan (me), Ebony and Ivory.

Today is a difficult day on the farm. **Water!!!** There are some air bubbles in the water that's pouring into the dam. I rebuild this 60 year old dam in two weeks; the sun is really getting hold of us, from six o'clock in the morning till six o'clock at night for two long weeks. We lay 50 millimeter in diameter plastic pipes for 200 meters in the sun, with a pick and shovel.

Dam builders, I'm taking the photo.

I have a 5000 liters water tank on a 5 meter tower for better water pressure that kept filled up permanently, just in case we get problems with the borehole, to make sure there's water for the house for at least 5 days. That will give us enough time to drill another bore hole, before the drinking waters finished, if there's money to drill another hole.

The dam has a capacity of 175 thousand liters of water that will last 7 days without a bore hole. When you see bubbles in your water falling into the dam, you know you have problems coming your way, low water level in the borehole. I remember the late nights sitting at the borehole, praying for water in those pipes. I kept on praying for about a week, because I knew there's no money for another borehole.

I mentioned the situation to the farm owner, with the hope that he will drill another borehole on his cost. No success, luckily his father came to my rescue. They drilled a hole about 10 meters from the house, 125 meters deep and 2500 gallons an hour, enough for my small land. The sad part of it, you will never know how long the borehole will last, but for the time being it will be all right, and there's no backup borehole.

Everything was back to normal in four days time. What's sad about this situation is the fact that you must stay positive all the time, it's not just water problems that attacks your self confidence. Problems with the workers, power failures, termites on the land you can't see, birds and monkey's eating strawberries. I had to shoot a monkey once a month to keep them of the land. The only way to get rid of birds is to cover your land with bird net.

WATER!!!

Termites: I remember walking in my strawberry land one day with my to border collies, Ebony and Ivory when I saw something unfamiliar wrong with some of the strawberry plants. I put my hand out to see why the leaves are lying so flat on the ground. I picked the plant up and found that there are no roots on it. Everything is gone, nothing, just the top part that's in the sun is left. A shock went threw me, the termites are eating anything that's not in the sun. They are busy attacking the roots of my strawberries.

There is only one way to save the strawberry land, poison. I went back to my house and get the mixture ready to pump it threw the system. You can't wait one hour, the termites will wipe your whole land out in a day or two. From then on, I looked after the termites once a week.

You need extra strength and income from somewhere, if you are a farmer. From the beginning as a farmer, I have started maintenance and hunting camp building business, there's always maintenance work on farm houses the farmers can't get to.

If I ever farm again, it will be a safari farm, wild animals that can help themselves for long periods of time. It's good to take your vehicle and drive through the bush to enjoy their way of living. It's keeping you young, and your mind away from the negative things that influence your life daily. Tomorrow you will feel good to start over again, solving problems . . . .

If you want to work in Africa you need to prepare yourself for the circumstances you are going to be in, and for the period you going to be in that spesific area. Remember, remember what you were told, it will help you to survive in the bush.

"Do your homework before you decide to go into certain areas in Africa."

"To know how to handle your rifle can save your life"

I took a friend and his son out on a hunting trip one week end, they were from the city, and the short weekend made it difficult to train and explain to them, where to look and what to do in the bush. I had to direct them while moving in the bush, what made it very difficult for hunting. Patience!!

There is one thing about a person that wants to hunt kudu for the first time with no hunting experience; they sometimes want to tell you what to do. 44 degrees in the sun is no joke. With plenty animals around us, we found nothing the first day. Sorry we found some, but when you see it, you must aim and shoot in seconds, otherwise, sorry! The next morning we are up early had a nice breakfast and a cup of coffee next to the campfire. Bags on the back, rifle over my shoulder, and off we went. We walked for the whole morning, at ten o clock I decided that we sit down for a break. We took our bags of our backs to get something for our dry mouths, and something to eat.

This morning I took a spoorsnyer with for an extra hand and eyes. We sat for about 15 minutes; I looked up straight into an oncoming kudu, not aware of us sitting in the lower grass. The spoorsnyer looked at me and I looked at him and I nod at him, our visitors are still busy with their snacks. I lifted the rifle slowly; it's so close I struggle to get focus in the scope, only ten feet away from us. I took aim at the neck and pulled the trigger, it fell like a dead kudu. Our guest jumped up and we calmed them down. What luck at ten o' clock in the morning? The spoorsnyer call on the radio for the vehicle to come for loading the kudu, and left us to get the vehicle at the dirt road.

I allow the father and son to sit next to the kudu for a photo session, without knowing that the kudu is still alive. I have cut the main blood supply on the neck and put him out for about 5 minutes. As the father and son moved away from the kudu it jumps up to get away from us into the bush, normally after a shot you reload immediately for just in case, I lifted my rifle and shot it in the run, it collapses for the second and last time. I will remember this for a long time and they will remember it forever.

There's nothing like fresh meat or liver on the campfire at night after a success full hunt, telling the stories in detail of the day's experience. Kudu in the cooler room and liver on the fire, and maybe an ice cold beer, or your favorite drink you brought along in the hand.

You see stars you haven't seen before, sounds you haven't heard before, fire you haven't seen or felt before, a picture only you will remember no camera can bring together in one snap. A picture with detail, only you will remember out of the angle you were sitting that night. Everyday is special day in the bushveld.

When you sit next to the fire you normally forget all the defects of the day and enjoy the moment you're in, after the weekend you make adjustments for the next expedition, but this night belongs to everybody in a positive sense, it's here to enjoy, because there is a kudu in the cooler room remember . . . .

Till late in the evening you will sit next to the campfire, because you know that you want to get maximum out of this evening, flames going nowhere, eating wood to survive. Tons of wood gets burned every year around campfires, and many books can get written about hunting stories under the African skies.

When you find tortes in the bush, you will know there is a place for any type of animal in the wilderness. You can walk in the bush without using your rifle, and learn so much with a bag full of patients.

If you can take a picture of a baobab tree, personally I think you must be one of the riches people in the world. Think about it, some of them are thousands of years old, and to capture that on one photo must be something special. It is something money can't buy; it's too old to connect it to money.

Nature gives us freedom you can't transfer to somebody else 100%, we must look after it, by only to leave our footprints behind. We take a lot away in our memories for many years. If you want to hunt, you hunt for only the meat you need to survive with.

Trophy hunting is a good thing if the meat goes to the people in need. But, the problem is that the hunter will pay for the hunt, and then the farmer will still sell the meat to the people in the community. So his getting double the amount for the specie that's been hunted.

I love New York, out of Africa into New York, what a mission. They driving on the wrong side of the road, then they use much bigger cars than other countries, bigger buildings, older buildings, wider streets for those bigger cars, more people, trains in tunnels, no smoking in buildings(nice), richer people, think big(nice), plenty snow(nice),

"Thank you for the people who took me to Vermont for my first ski trip on thanksgiving weekend, I enjoyed it like a toddler." "For Tanya who helped me after a couple of serious out of control slides down the mountain." I think I looked like a rabbit biting its ankles in a yellow jacket. Luckily no one else had a yellow jacket, so they could keep their eyes on me, a nice looking girl for a trainer. Born with a good balance, I tackled the black diamond on the third day, meaning the highest point of the mountain. I'M FROM AFRICA, remember, we tackle mountains with the bare hand and a rifle on the back in 40-50 degrees in the sun, and we do without skis.

I cooked my first turkey in America, and enjoy it after wards; the smell of the chutney mixture and turkey will stay in my memory for ever. I like the idea of the turkey on thanksgiving weekend in America, great idea America. *In Africa we use the ostrich.* (Joke)

I have made a decision to sign this book to people in "NEW YORK" in a nice coffee shop, a coffee shop with a taste for good coffee. Even if I sit there for a whole month and sign my book every day, I will do so.

I have learned one thing about the American people, **think big**, and keep on doing so. I went back to South Africa with something I believed before I went over to America. Think big, but I had to see it for myself; if they can do it surely I can do it as well. Only one thing in South Africa, you need people with a **think big mind** to support you, and that is difficult to get . . . .

I missed South Africa for the time I have been in America. The thorn trees, the open African skies, stars you can nearly touch, it's like a ceiling for the poor, for those that don't have money to put a ceiling in their little shelter, for those who must sit around the fire outside their shelters where they cook their food every night. I think is for them, *the number people.*

It took me a while to get used to no fences around the houses in America, no electric fencing, glory. I like, I like, America, but the bush is much better, the baobab, thorn, lead wood, and njala tree. Camp fire, camp fire!!!!

It's always good to be back in your own country, leave your country only if you have to. Sadly in South Africa it's the case for many white South Africans, and they are still leaving the country because of politics and crime. My opinion, one culture can't rule over another culture. You can learn that from the animal kingdom. The lion thinks his in control, till he gets involved with a couple of buffalo's, then he will not see tomorrow. With the wrong angle anything can go in a negative direction.

Many people lost their lives because of people ruling over people with a wrong angle. It's good to stay to your basic way of living, don't worry you will get to the winning line, those who run past you, you will pick some of them up on your way, that's if they are still alive. Nobody must start a marathon on high speed; they will surely not make it.

I mentioned earlier that I use to build hunting camps and restorations on farm houses . . . The second farm we lived on, I had to rebuild this sixty odd year old house before we could move in, this is also the house where I rebuild the dam I was telling you about. (Put some photo's in, so that you can get a better picture of my story about the bushveld)

Before

After

Before

After

It took me many months to rebuild this house for us to live in. even after we moved in, I was still busy fixing it . . . I think God blessed me with a straight string connected from my eyes to my brain, what I see I can normally do, or I can quickly make a plan on the spot. I like to be a winner over practical situations.

If you want to survive you must push forward, and sometimes quickly. I saw some of those old buildings in New York with the stairs coming down the outside of the walls, and thought by myself, I can take one of these buildings, and change them into something AFRICAN a New Yorker hasn't seen before. Imagine my own building in New York; it will be a "WOW" feeling.

I like buildings, hope to have my own shopping centre one day (BIG ONE)

We must learn to be an answer to other people's problems, to create new ideas people sitting on, and they don't even know it.

One of the successes in life is to keep on going, even if it takes you twenty odd years. Look at Colonel Saunders the Kentucky Uncle, nobody wanted to help him, and till one day he caught the big fish. **No 2** is to get the rite team together for your vision, you can make adjustments, but let no one tamper with your heart desire. It's yours and keep it that way. Let them understand what you want in life.

There are many people sitting like vultures, ready to snatch your vision. Be aware of them.

Make sure that your vision will last a hundred years, so if you don't start it, it will not last, and many people in the future will not be able to live of it. Always remember your homework.

Just think of your family that will follow after you. You can look after them for many years to come. Think of the businesses in your own country, some of the people that have started some of those businesses aren't there anymore, but because of their decisions, they are still looking after people today, and maybe for many years that will follow.

Life's full of choices, and we have to make a choice and stay with it, even if you go down without doing your homework. You will learn, and then you will stand up much stronger than before, and much wiser. (Do your homework)

HOW Could anybody take a chance week after week buying lotto tickets, but for their heart desire that's much more worth than lotto, they do nothing to start maybe one of the biggest businesses in their country.

While fixing the second house, I build a veranda at the back door with a big braai area (area for gathering on weekends to barbeque on the open coal). I build it big enough to put a whole middle size pig or duiker on, especially when we get visitors from the city.

NICE, BELIEVE ME . . . .

I will go out the day before, to shoot the pig, and let it hang after John cleaned it nicely, till it's cold for the next day.

I will start the fire with thorn tree wood and build up a nice heap of thorn tree coal, before I put the pig onto the spit, I will stuffed it with bacon and sheep fat, just to give it a nice taste and then it's not too dry. Because the pigs got a very dry meat, I will make a special sauce to put onto the pig with a brush while it's turning over the hot thorn tree coal. To give it a nice shiny color and a little sweetie taste, I paint some Marula jelly over it. Marula jelly is a fruit you get in some areas in Africa.

We made it part of our business for extra income to make jelly out of it, and sell it with various other jams, including strawberry and gooseberry jam to businesses in the city. Marula is a fruit with a very high pectin percentage when it's green, off cause a whole cooking process to get to the final product. You can put it on bread, and any other kind of food you like to put it in. It's very sweet. I can make the nicest beer out of the marula fruit. A beer you will never forget.

While the pigs on the turn, I will prepare another sauce that will go into small sauce cups you will find next to your plate where you will dip your meat in, before eating it. With that I will make finally sure that you don't eat dry meat.

"This barbeque will take you past twelve at night."

You will get homemade bread, Marula jelly and potato salad with it. And for desert, strawberries you dip in hot chocolate yourself. I promise you, this is one meal you will never forget.

Snake again; one of these well planed evenings got delayed for a half an hour, when I hurt one of the dogs (the female) made a soft grr noise, then you know you can get your shotgun and spotlight, you must know your dogs, they can safe your live, only if you know their ways. I ran quickly into the house and gripped the light and shotgun; they are normally in one place.

I called Ivory further away from the area where she saw the snake. I bought these two border collies as puppies and trained them every day. If I whistle or call they will listen immediately.

I gave the spot light to a bushveld friend to spot the snake, so that I can get the shotgun to my shoulder for the shot. You must never take a change with any snake, as he spotted the snake; I pulled the trigger, and shot the snake. The snake traveled through the air as if blown by the wind, Mozambican spitting cobra, sorry.

You must leave a snake after you have shot it, so that the dogs can smell it, it's a way to make them more aware of snakes.

We enjoyed our evening, and again the pig on the spit, made it a happy evening.

Strawberries dipped in hot chocolate sauce, what better way to end a snake interfered evening . . . *I LOOOVE STRAWBERRIES!!!!!!!*

One morning John came with the news that there must be a snake somewhere in the yard, because they could only find the incoming spoor and not the outgoing spoor. Puff adder he said.

We normally start from one side of the yard to the other side, to make sure we cover the whole yard. Not everybody will look for snakes, only the men, they are well trained to look for snakes, and once they found it they will call me to shoot it.

A puff adder they normally hit with a knob kierie (cane), they found this puff adder next to the garage under the gas bottles. John sorted the snake out with a kierie and Jonathan (18 months) my son took over.

PUFF ADDER!!!

Rain in the bushveld, it's like manna from heaven. I like rain. Walk in it like a child. You can't buy water with all the money in the world, water, one of two sources on earth that brings forth live on earth, the other one, the sun. The photos will give you an idea of rain once in a hundred years in the bushveld.

It's good to see the rain drops falling on the leaves, and the smell off the earth in your nostrils, a smell you can't forget.

In the bushveld you pray for rain every sunny day.

If you look at your life, you must see it as a steppingstone towards the bigger picture. A steppingstone will take you closer to the garden where you can enjoy life in full. So don't give up, whatever crosses your path, just don't lose your grip on your vision. Remember it's yours, keep it, and don't ever give it up. Stick to your vision like glue to glue.

If you have no vision, you better find your heart's desire, otherwise you will be a slave to somebody else's vision and never be 100% happy in your life, unless it's part of your vision.

A vision can be big or small, doesn't matter, you will be happy there most of the times, but at least you will be on your right place on earth.

What makes life difficult, other people's opinions about your decisions'? Listen to them and take the positive out of it to build your vision. I like critics, it builds my vision.

I need only dream makers in my life, people with a supporting attitude. So you get two kinds of people, dream makers and dream breakers, you can choose who you wants to walk the walk with, at the end you will pay for the losses, or bank the profit.

I am not one of these big African hunters, but whenever I'm in the bush with a rifle, I hunt for meat only; I will use the opportunity to enjoy it to its maximum, the sun, the trees, the insects, and just to be there, to be part of nature, whether you find something to hunt or not. Sitting on some of those rocks on the mountain, drinking in nature as far as the eye can see, is not transferable in words.

I like to write this book, because it must look after somebody when I'm not there in the future. Every living sole on earth is like a book on two feet, but nobody will know your story, unless you put it on paper. Even if it takes you a couple of years, just put it on paper it's good for your soul.

Some of you will know that the riches place in any town will always be the graveyard. Why? Because many people lying there wanted to do something when they were alive, but never did. There are so many dreams in grave yards. Paintings, cars, books, houses, jobs, etc. never came to life. **Don't be selfish to take your dream to your grave**, leave it behind to look after someone that stays behind.

We must remember one thing every day of our lives, our life on earth is only temporary, and not for ever. So, do what you know you suppose to do, and work hard to do well, without harming other people, rather look after them than harming them.

In the bushveld some boys will shoot their first kudu between five and eight years old. They will handle a rifle from four years old and become natural hunters you won't believe. They will start shooting pigeons guineefowls, rabbits, duiker, warthog, impala and then the kudu, blouwildebeest, till they can hunt the biggest of them all, the eland.

What makes them such good hunters? The particle training and discipline their fathers apply onto their children. The farmer will take their children into the bush from an early age. I took Jonathan to the bush in my vehicle on seven weeks, and he learned a lot, just by hearing and seeing over a period.

I still need to tell you about the biggest warthog I have shot, next to the maize land.

Like usual I parked my vehicle a good distance from the maize land, we walk to the same tree for shade where I shot my first warthog. We took exactly the same spot, so that we can see left and right side without missing any warthog coming out of this maize land.

It's hot today; you need a hat everyday in the bushveld, most of the times you will recognize someone on the hat his wearing. No hat and you won't have the sun burn the skin of your ears.

We have been sitting in the sun for about 2 hours, thinking about things you don't have time to think of when you are busy on the farm.

You won't believe what happens to you when you see two of the biggest warthogs you have ever seen, appears at about forty meters from you. 5 seconds, that's all you've got to pick one aim and shoot. These big warthogs are well trained in nature, you don't see these size very often, it's the first and last time I saw a monster warthogs like this.

I lifted my rifle in two seconds, and put big one in focus, right on the heart and pulled the trigger. The warthog ran right through the next farmers fence that's about four meters from where I have shot it, and collapsed six meter on the other side' of the fence. John ran and climb over the fence in one movement, he pulled the warthog back to the fence and we both pulled it back into the area where I have shot it.

I left John with the warthog while I went to bring the pickup closer; I haven't seen a size of warthog like this in my life. I parked the pickup as close as possible to the warthog; it took us much longer as the previous once to get It onto the back of the pickup. We looked at it after we have loaded it. Unbelievable but true.

This warthog I shot for myself. It weighs 80 kilograms after we have cleaned it, it weighs 52 kilograms. See photo;

I let the butcher made some Russian saurgages, steaks and mince meat for many months.

There is something that happens with you when you lift a rifle after you have spotted the animal you want to bring down, something you can't explain, something you must feel for yourself. I can tell you one thing, it's a good feeling, different like sex, and it's also a different world you can't explain to someone else, you must be there to feel it, be part of it, you must do it. Remember it's not just for men, women are good hunters too, and some of them are beautiful, and how.

If you ever come to Africa on safari, you must try, if possible to climb into a baobab tree, just for the experience of it, a feeling you can take with you into your future. Something you can tell over as a story to your children and friends. It's good to see a baobab tree, but much better to climb in it; it gives you a richer experience.

Many people want to hunt something in the bush, but because they never handled a rifle they don't do it. You are welcome to ask a hunter to take you out on a small expedition where he can do the hunting on your behalf, but the difference in this situation is that you will always be with him right where the action will take place. I call it, "PARTNER SHOOTING"

If you ever want to hunt "PARTNER SHOOTING" you make sure you contact me for a "BUSH" experience you will never forget. BUSH CAMP, CAMP FIRE, AFRICAN SKIES AND SOUNDS. Don't forget the food. Yum, Yum!!

You will be taken through the whole hunting process, and you will get into a baobab tree, that I promise you. You can even plant a tree in AFRICA with your name and planting date on it. A way to leave something behind for Africa's future. One tree can help birds, can give fruit to animals, and can give shade to a kudu one day. What about oxygen?

There is many ways to look after our planet, if everybody can do just a small bit, we will save it for our followers.

Yes-yes-yes!!!!

We are in a life situation where there are a lot of changes going on worldwide. We need to bring some of the basics back on earth to save some part of it.

In **South Africa, we need to look after our water. How? We need a private sector team to take it over. People that's qualified to do the work. People that know the bigger picture and that can do something about it.**

Farmers **are wiping out our nature, by using too much water out of boreholes. The roots of the bigger trees can't get to the water anymore, because of water levels dropping so much that their roots can't get to the water anymore. The rain water is not enough to keep them alive during the year. Africa leaders need to discipline the farmer more in South Africa. Tons of food got thrown away daily, it means,**

not much control over the way farmers are doing it. See it's about money, and not about saving water.

Frost on the tomato land;

I have planted this nice patch of tomatoes (with help off 'cause). Giving water every day, looking how they grow. Counting the days for the picking date, make financial sums. Work out the profit. Not much but it will be something to stay alive for a month or so. Waiting, waiting, for the big day, every day in the land, waiting for yellow flowers to come, plenty of them. Every flower means a tomato, and I know there will be more than enough. The yellow flowers came and went, and in their place came this thing called a tomato, what a good feeling to see some changes in nature. A fruit, many people is under the impression that it's a vegetable.

I can still remember the green tomato smell, I smelt every day in that land. My first time I have ever planted tomato and it's looking like a great success, success, the way I am feeling at that stage, good. BUT . . . .

You can take from nature and survive while you are on this planet, but winning it, I don't know, nature will have the last say over this body it fed over the years, it will go back to dust my friend. Nature gives you room to learn from it.

Natures never negative, it allows you to feed of it day after day, isn't it wonder full? BUT . . . .

Sometimes you will make it, and then there are times you have to make peace and carry on with another planting project. BUT . . . .

Two weeks before starting to pick my first tomatoes I have ever planted. It was a normal day like any other winters day in the Bushveld, you know, like giving water to the most beautiful tomato plants on this planet, my first ever. So the day end like any other winters day in the bushveld, just to remind you, you can plant whole year (twelve month) in the bushveld, with maybe two nights of frost, and just some tears. But this time, it came like a thief in the night.

I got up early the next morning (6 am.) and could feel the difference in temperature when I got out of the house. I looked at the tomato land that's about twenty meters from the house, everything looks in place, and there is some frost on the lawn, but the tomato's looks very well. BUTT . . . .

I could see the sun is coming up in the east, like all the other mornings, thorn trees on the horizon, like the beginning of any other day. BUTT . . . .

At seven o'clock I could see the sun in full. The way I know nature is, that the sun is energy, and it must help plants to grow, and make branches longer, and leaves bigger. BUTTTTT, not this morning, not on my tomato land. Every plant went down, down, down, down, till it was lying flat on the surface of the life giving earth.

When I saw that tomato land that early morning, every plant were frozen, and I couldn't see it. I didn't know the sign of coming frost, I should've seen the previous afternoon.

We pulled out all those tomato plants and put in beans. At least we made something out of them.

Somebody once said; a farmer is like street women, they know they do wrong, but they just carry on. (Only a joke, okay. We can't survive without farmers.)

I have leaned one thing about life on this planet, I can't be perfect. But with everything you do, keep an honest heart, even if people don't believe in what you are doing, just keep your heart honest.

We must move on, weather people agree or not, if you listen to others and it doesn't work, they will just back off, and you will carry the loss. So, do your homework, and if it doesn't work, you are the only one to blame for.

Every day you put your feet out of bed onto this planet, it will always be change you took to go into this day. Problems will always be there, be an answer to it. Keep on trying till you get the upper hand over your daily problems, and you will not get it right the first or second day, but good leaders will carry on till they become winners over their problems.

I will never forget my tomato land, but I have made peace over the situation quickly as possible. I had to; leaders make peace, no peace no leader. Remember the dream maker dream breaker, a leader will always be supporting in other people's dreams. Leaders will always handle their own crisis situation in a more positive way than non leaders. Don't get me wrong, anybody can be a leader, but you have to make a decision to become one. This leadership is a long training session, your whole life, and the best way to become a good leader will always be the practical way. Don't forget the theoretical side, it must be there, but the practical side makes you a solid leader. People in need, need some food on the table, not a book.

My farm workers need meat on their table today, not how God created it, that I can tell them later, by telling them will bring nothing in their stomach. Most of the time a leader will do something in a practical way to help people.

Easy test, go into the poor area and give someone a news paper, then give someone a meal, and find out which one of the two will be the happiest, then you build the result into your life for your own future.

My first kudu;

I stayed in friends hunting camp on a farm called Amatola (I think it means kudu in the mountain) the farm is just next to the saltpans on the northern side of the soutpansberg mountain. He owes about 3, 000 hectors on the mountain side and two third off the farm is mountain area. He build a camp very close to the mountain and a about 50 meters from a dam wall been build in the second world war by the Italian convicts by rock that's been found in the area.

You will find nice dome tents on cement slabs walking area paved out with mountain rock, kitchen with freezer to keep your meet and drinks cool. The kitchen is build by rock, one meter high, and further up its covered with wire mesh to keep the monkey's and baboons out. Baboons can clean your kitchen out in ten minutes, and nobody wants that in the bush.

I slept over one night to look for my first kudu the next morning. At about 5.30 am. I took my rifle hanged it over my right shoulder and decided to walk close to the mountain in an eastern direction. Also the time the kudu's will come down from the mountain to feed on the flat area where they will find tree's to feed on. Kudu normally feeds on trees.

I'm alone in the bush, only rifle and two way radio. I don't take a bag with when I'm alone, only when there's a person with me that's not fit enough to last for 4-5 hours in the sun. The two way radio for emergency, or for a success hunt. Make sure to take a water canteen every time you go into the bush. You don't take any chances with the bushveld sun, it will take any moist it can get out of your body. When you realize it, it could be too late.

I walked as quiet as possible through the bush till I reach the foot of the mountain, then you reach the open area where your chances to be seen is a ninety present, kudu is very accurate to spot you from a far distance. If a kudu sees you he or she will give one bark, more a less like a dog sound, then all of them will run in different directions, and you will get nothing to shoot at.

But this morning I walked like another animal, eyes on the mountain and rifle ready to lift and aim in seconds. I knew this is the time for them to come down, and will find one if I'm not too much on my nerves. Everything must be in place, the wind directions that's one of the most important parts of nature to take in consideration, most of the time the wind will come up round about ten o'clock.

I walked about five hundred meters, when my eye saw a movement about 70 meters up the mountain. It's a kudu coming down the mountain to start another day in the bush area. The kudu will go every evening round about 17h00 to the mountain where they know they could feel safe.

I lifted my rifle very slowly in a standing position, the kudu is still moving downwards. I took aim just little bit higher on the shoulder us usual, because of the uphill. I can feel the tension in my body, my first kudu will I bring it down or . . . ,

I just pulled the trigger without thinking any more. The kudu dropped like a kudu on that very spot.

What an ice breaker. So I got my first kudu in one hour because of the fact that I knew their way. We enjoyed the kudu meat for many months. Hunt only what you need, or hunt for someone else what they need to survive with.

Most of my hunting I've done on the Amatola farm. Love to walk in the bush on Amatola; I have learned many from this friend of mine. He grew up in this bush, and if you see him misses something, you will be very lucky. His very short person and short tempered to round the shortness of. One of the best persons to learn from. Doesn't miss anything, from sounds till any movement an animal will make. Not perfect, but good. You can never be perfect in the bush, it's their territory, and you can only learn some of the ways of the wild. You will get close, but never hundred percent, you must accept it, and make peace with it.

I got so fast with the .303, if I misses a warthog the first shot, I will reload and bring it down on the second or third bullet in the run, and believe me, once start running they already on high speed, remember, I trained on them to shoot any animal in the run.

Why I'm telling you this? Remember I was telling about the hunting camps and restoration business I was doing part time? One ugly day crossed my path one day I didn't want, as a matter of fact, I don't think anybody on earth wanted something like this that happened to me that specific day.

While putting kitchen cupboards into a kitchen, you know with all this dangerous machines around you, anything can turn negative in seconds, and change your live around in seconds you didn't planned for.

While working with one of these machines, I ask my helper to take good grip on the piece of wood I need to trim with my circular saw. He slipped while I'm busy cutting the piece of wood, my reaction is to stop the wood coming to my side with my right hand while the machine still in 2000+ revolutions. I pushed my hand right into the running blade. Because it was a rough blade it smashed my fingers and looks like a cracker blown it up. The blade went through four fingers except for the thump. The blade went 90 percent through my middle and ring finger, halfway through the inner side of the two fingers sides of the middle and ring finger. I lost a piece of meat on the outside of the pinky.

Luckily for me the owner of the house were on the premises. He drove me to the nearest hospital. On duty was one of the best doctors everybody knew him for his accurate work. He worked my fingers back to where it belongs. Because I never smoked in my life I only visited him twice. The very next day I took the same machine and build a corner toilet role holder, just to get my brain over this yesterday disaster.

It took me two hours to build the three compartment toilet role holder, but I can assure you, it helped me to get over this situation in one day, and ready for my hunting expedition.

This is the reason I were telling you this, I have organized a hunting trip months ago for that very next week, taking out a father and son on a weekend for a hunting experience in the bush. If you know me better you will know it takes a lot to stop me from doing something I have planned.

I had this big bandage on my right hand, so I have to get rid of some of it, and then, I need a trigger finger. I opened the trigger finger with three stitches in it, and decided it's not so pain full. Now there are only three fingers in a smaller bandage. Now for the practice round, to make sure I can shoot accurately and reload in time, just in case I miss the first time.

My Amatola friend stood with me next to the practice bench. I put the rifle on the bench, cross on the target; I can feel the pain in my hand when I started to pull the trigger closer towards me with that half-cut finger. As soon as the shot went off, the rifle kicked back into my damaged hand. I shot another three shots, and decided I'm ready for this bush. I'm here to shoot a kudu, and kudu I'm going to get.

Because of my hand, I have organized two spoorsnyers, one for myself, and one to take the father and son on their hunting expedition.

I would see my spoorsnyer for the last time on that hunting trip, because of HIV/AIDS, maybe his one of the HIV/AIDS patients that caused me to make a decision later in my life to help the HIV/AIDS patient's food wise worldwide. **That's why part of the profit of this book will go to HIV/AIDS patients worldwide.**

We walk through the bush in absolute silence, but this time it's different, every hundred to two hundred meters the spoorsnyer will take a rest to take

Some water in. I know him for many years that are why I picked the change up early in the walk.

It took us longer, but his still accurate in his work. It took us two hours to get our first kudu. I put the cross right on the kudu like the first one in the mountain, little bit lower because I'm not shooting uphill this time, but in the lower bush area. The only thing I've got after the shot is a handful of pain and no kudu. I missed it on a distance of forty meters. Damn.

We walked for another hour till we got the second kudu, not one but four to six of them, I must make a quick decision which one I want to shoot takes me only seconds to do so, because of the bush I need to make a quick decision. I put the telescope on the chosen one and pulled the trigger, I missed it, I reload shoot misses again, reload aim shoot for the third time, I shot the kudu in the run on the right spot, the kudu game down and we could see the dust as the hundred and twenty kilogram kudu body hits the ground full speed. I send a bullet out every five meters while that kudu were running. Pain in the hand, what pain?????

It's good to be back at camp, you could feel the long walk in your body when you sit down in a camping chair with a cold drink in the hand. My left hand feels heavier as well, wonder why.

That evening you could feel the positive calmness in the atmosphere around the camp fire. The visitors shot a warthog during their trip, gives them also something to be positive about. They recon they hurt a machine gun while I tried to get the kudu down. That night, pain in the hand, what pain?????

We are enjoying the stories, while looking at the flames till late in the night. Life's about different angles, same thing, and different stories.

Another day on the farm, I'm not feeling well today, but you will know when you are working for yourself in any business, there is no time for laying low.

If you're the person with the vision full of ideas, then you must pick your body up and go out there to let it happens. Every defect on the farm or any business will always come back to you; you will always be the responsible person, no matter what. Your workers can come and go, but you will always be there with something very special, your vision. If there are big profits it will also come to you. You're the boss. (Dream maker remember)

It's good to be a vision carrier. It places you in a position to change the world for many people around you, not for all of them, but for some.

Once you're out in the strawberry land or bush, you tense to feel better in a way. Tonight I can go to bed earlier to have a good rest for the next they, and hopefully in a better condition.

I'm not the type of person that can handle heat, give me ice and I'm happy. In the summer time I will sleep with a fan next to my bed, on a maximum speed till the next morning. It keeps my temperature down, and helps to keep the mosquitoes away from me. Another problem in Africa, as most of you knows. You get the big five in Africa, but you can add the mosquito to make it the big six. The mosquito killed more people in Africa than any other animal, and still doing so. And it's an insect, and much smaller than all of them.

The sound of a mosquito can keep you awake for many hours at night. Sorry, for those without mosquito's repellent in a bush camp.

The BUSHVELD is like a bread basket for poor people, whether you're a white or black person. Farmers will always allow you to take some of the crop they have planted. Those they know they can't send to the fresh market, from potatoes, watermelons, sweet corn, peppers, onions, mangos, oranges ext. So it's cheap to live in a farming community. But a future, I'm not so sure. If you can't control your own selling price, you will always have financial problems.

Farmers must get sorted out; you can't just plant what you want to plant. This is a discussion not for this book. At this moment you can't tell a farmer what to do. If somebody is not going to do something very quickly, they will pump all the water out of the bore holes till the last drop. All that matters day after day, they must make more money. ***SORRY FOR THE FUTURE!!***

Let me give you a nice recipe you can use on any hind, let's call it the: "BUSHVELD SPECIALITY"

To start with, you need the following,
One wine glass, (for yourself)
Fill the glass with wine to the top.
One bottle of your choice wine, (for yourself)
Put the bottle of wine in a cool place, not too far away from the working place.
If you don't enjoy making food, you get me, so that you can only watch and eat . . . .
One spit or oven.
1 Hind unfrozen,
1 sheep tale, or 20 pieces of curled bacon,
10 baby carrots,
20 sugar cherries

If it's pig you use sheep tale fat, cut in 10 mm pieces, push a sharp knife into the meat right to the centre bone.

Push the pieces of cut tale into the holes with your finger as deep as possible, fifteen to twenty holes. You must stuff it like a bushveld cook. If you can't, you get me to do it.

If it's sheep hind, you use curled up bacon.

Do the same with ten baby carrots

To add some style and little bit of sweetness, do the same with sugar cherry's.

Put your oven on a temperature of 140 degree while you prepare the cover sauce.

Now what will we paint this piece of meat with? If you don't have any MARULA jelly, I will bring along if you want me to do it, otherwise you take:

*1*x50 mm clean meat brush,
200 grams apricot jam,
200 grams fruit chutney,
200 mil of your choice of wine,
Salt, enough,
Black or white pepper,
200 mil good oil,

Mix the ingredients with a medium spoon till you are sure the apricot jams not visible.

When your oven temperature reaches 140 degrees you pour half of your mixture over the meat.

Put your meat into the oven and paint it with the left over mixture every 15 minutes.

Turn the meat every 30 minutes and paint it directly after the turning process.

The apricot and fruit chutney will give the meat a nice brown and shiny color.

When it's ready according to the way you want it, you can dish it up with rice, nice mixed vegetables. You can heat the left over sauce up and use it for a sauce over the rice.

Cut slices of +-10 mm, depends on how many of you want to tackle the piece of meat.

If you need some pudding, remember the strawberry dipped in chocolate. Always a winner or even different kind of fruit can also do. Never forget the hot chocolate. You will stay a star for many years because of one night. Enjoy.

If you think you will not come right, fly me in to make sure of a nice piece of meat. **Enjoy!!!**

I'm not fussy when it comes to food; struggle to get olives into my body. Grew up to poor as a child to be fussy over food.

I will never be fussy when somebody gives me food I don't like; I would rather leave it in silence.

Why fussy about food if so many people die in Africa with, maybe one meal a day. How is it possible that so many people can die in Africa, one of the riches continents in the world? Easy, cut unqualified and greedy politicians out, and bring more private companies in with a well structured food plan with their business plan. The western world is taking too much and leave not enough positive behind to look after the owners of Africa. **Who are they? The people on the streets of Africa!!!!!!**

I worked with some of these poor people, not even a voice, just a human being living from one day to another. Never learned to plan for tomorrow. It will not help them, because there's nothing to planned for.

Today is a new day, a day with sunshine you just get in the bushveld, sweaty and at least two shirts today. At mid day you will put a fresh shirt on. Sweat and dust will change your shirts color in six hours.

Every day is well planned from the human side. But, there will always be the elements from the side that will interfere.

Walking through the gooseberry land, noticing that there is something not in place. There's a lot of gooseberry's lying between the lanes on the ground.

As I picked one of the cups up I notice that there is no fruit inside the cup. Every cup I picked up is fruitless. Rats are eating the gooseberries at night, and they love the fruit.

Plan a; I cut 110 mm in diameter plastic pipes in 500 mm lengths, mix some poison with maize meal and put the mixture in the pipes. Reason for the pipes, so that we can prevent the birds for spotting the maize.

To make double sure we only put the pipes out at the evening when we know the rats are active. We remove the pipes with the poison early in the morning. Did we pick up rats every morning? It carried on for about two weeks. We surely wiped them out in that area around the gooseberry land. Plan a worked.

***What* will the bushveld be without:** a sweaty body day after day, head without a hat, feet without boots on it, farmer without a pickup, people without visions, area without a thorn, baobab and njala tree, camp fire in the bush and meat on the fire? **NOTHING!!!**

2010 one of the farmers I knew, shot himself accidently. Apparently he went out to the land on the Sunday morning with his rifle. When he got home he walked to the safe to put his rifle away while talking to his wife. As he put the rifle in the safe a shot went off, the bullet went right through his neck, killing him instantly in front of his wife. Good person, he grew up in the bushveld with rifles. But if you don't put your rifle on safe, you could get problems sooner or later, father of three children, and still in school. He died in the house he grew up in. I have done some restoration work on his house a couple of years ago, and got to know him for two weeks. A solid bushvelder.

It's sad to lose a farmer in any country. They are looking after many people all over their own country and even in the world. Take the farmers away and you take your food basket away.

Phone call from Amatola farm, eland shot in the mountain. An American hunter shot an eland high in the mountain round about 3 in the afternoon. This means late evening in the mountain to night. Don't think you shoot anything like the size of an eland in the mountain and try to move it down the mountain without a struggle.

We got about 300 meters from the eland with the pick-up at about 4 pm. We were still busy at 9pm that night, lying on the rocks looking at the stars of Africa, while the workers are loading the meat on the pick-up, overtime payment for them.

The workers had to skin the eland and carried 700kg of meat in the darkness of Africa, piece by piece to the pick-up. Not easy task. If you ever shoot any animal in the mountain, know that your tariff will be much higher, at least extra five workers just to move your hunt down the mountain.

You only take 700 kg eland, eight people on and in a Toyota Hi-lux pick-up downhill in the dark if you know what you're doing. The road is build with mountain rock by hand many years ago. If you go more than 5 km per hour on these loose rocks, you will not make the foot of the mountain on wheels. We went up about 7 km; it took us another one and a half hour to get the eland to the cooler.

No meat on the
Campfire tonight. Damn!!!

If I don't write anything about the HIV/AIDS situation in Africa in this book, I will miss something special to tell you to make you more aware of people nobody knows about. About people that die every day, people with nothing on their name. People that worked for me, and people I worked with in the bush. I need to reveal something that boost HIV/AIDS in South Africa you won't believe. **Minimum wage without homework!!**

The government brought minimum wage in on farms. Good idea, BUT . . .

A normal farm set up with your workers, works as follows. The farmer will identify and appoint one of the workers with some leadership and a person the others will listen to if you give him work instruction for his team. The workers will get a salary every two weeks or once a month with a 25 kg bag of maize per month.

The leader will get 2/3 to double the amount of wage more than the normal workers. The other workers admire him for the amount of wage his getting, why?

Because, he can pay for a women staying (sleep with) with him that can do all his cooking and washing during the month, something the others can't do. He can go out and pay any other women to sleep with, if he wants to, and the other workers can't, they don't get enough money to do so.

Then one day the S.A government announced the minimum wage on farms. The wage must double, and the workers must buy their own food for the month. The farmers were very cross for this government's decision. **But,** then the problems with the HI/AIDS moved in. the moment the workers waited for, to pay for something they saw everyday they couldn't get, **WOMEN!!!**, and the women were ready for them. Where there's money you will find women, and they are willing to take all the men with money they can get. Women need to survive as well, in the bushveld more men will get work than women, men can work harder, and they get more money. The woman will get casual work in the picking season and handle the men at night time, extra money.

You could see how good men and women went down in a very short time. The four immediate reasons for wiping out this people, **1)** no training how to handle more money, **2)** women, **3)** can't look after themselves, no more buying food for the whole month, **4)** and the killer that take away all their control, **ALCOHOL!!!**

We can't stop this killer decease, but we can make a difference in some of these people's lives, **training**, from the farmer down to the farm worker.

I personally think we can make a big deference in the daily living of farm workers. **Planning!!!** To implement a well structured basic plan. **Better way of living**.

People believe in medicine to help these patients, not bad idea. If you are lying in hospital they will give you food before you get medicine. How does the medicine supplier know the patient is following a balanced diet????

To see someone perish in Africa because of HIV/AIDS is much deferent than on other continents, the reason for the deference, **POVERTY**. Here they mostly die because of no balanced food daily; they can't get the right amount of food in their body to build their immune system to prevent this killer decease to take them down.

I'm no medical doctor, but I lived and worked with them daily in the bush and saw how they lived a life most of the 1st world is not aware of. To live and work with people is to understand them. We are not allowing saying something about other people's circumstances unless we are part of it for a while, you must feel their feel, and live their way of living. We need to live with these people to know and understand their need, and mostly their cry for answers on the practical side of their lives (food, clothes and a better future for his/her family.) there is nothing in place for these peoples future, just another day.

How will anybody know their circumstances if somebody don't tell the outside world about the ground level crisis? Not to sell my book, but to make more people aware of people in a situation most people don't know of, and don't want to be in, to rather use some of this books profit to invest into a food project for HIV/AIDS patients worldwide. Know your status!!!

HIV/AIDS is no more just a country decease, but a worldwide crises. We need constant money to help these patients. It's a good thing to give money to help them, but it will be much better if the givers can invest in businesses, to create a financial fountain that can bring constant capital in, to look after HIV/AIDS patient's food wise.

Life must be like a scale in any persons mind, the practical and the theory must hang equal to understand any situation. Too much people will tell a story about people with only half the truth. If you get the theory, and then you must find the practical and make sure you understand it, don't just find it, we must understand it, before we can say anything about it.

Let's think about this for a moment, a person has HIV and he knows it, live by maize daily with meat some days, cabbage and water, he knows his on his way out. He's a DAD and HUSBAND, what will he leave behind for his family to carry on with. Some of them live in such a fear because of this one reason,

what I can leave behind for my family to live with, (normally nothing.)

Question: how can this Continent called Africa with so many riches in about everything, turn out to be so poor when you look at his people? Well sorry to say, mostly greedy **POLITITIONS.** Most of the politicians in Africa are overweight, and their supporters underfed. Make your sum, and there are many sums to be made.

Let me tell you about Philamon; a young man, age twenty six. I saw this young well build worker one year before he died, working for a farmer with something we don't want. Please keep in mind all of these African people are working for money (survival). They are not there for the farmer, so the farmer feels the same way, his on his farm to make money and not there for the workers. If you can do the work, you're in, and it will sometimes cost you your life to stay in.

Philamon was a good and hard worker, work as a normal farm worker, if there's a gap you must fill it, weather it in the potato land, packing of the potato's or digging trenches. Most of the workers must be all rounder's, if you're an all rounder, you are more secure of your work position. We never spoke one word during that year till the last day he got onto my vehicle.

I did see Philamon during his last year, always part of the working team. Then for about 3 months I haven't seen him, I got busy building a hunting camp that kept me busy for a couple of months.

One day I met the farmer while his team was digging a drain for one of his houses. We were busy in a conversation, when I heard this funny coughing from one of the workers, and in the middle of the summer in the bushveld you don't cough, as I turned around to spot the person with the cough, I looked straight in a skinny face I hardly recognize, Philamon. I looked at the farmer and he just pulled his shoulders up, then I knew, Philamon is on his way out, and he knows it.

I took Philamon to a clinic, but to get Philamon onto my pick up, two of my workers had to help me to get him on, and support him till we reached the clinic.

Sadly Philamon only lived for another two weeks. **Another voting number gone!!**

One person on a farm can get trained to help his own people, maybe with extra salary per month. They can put a union member on the farm, but what about a trained hiv/aids supporter? **Just a question**.

One big problem in Africa will always be the truck drivers. The women know they have cash especially for them. Take a truck drivers cash away and you will help to prevent spreading hiv/aids in a way. These people don't care for each other, the one want sex and the other one cash, and they will push their bodies till the limits.

I remember the time in Zambia, as you walk through the bush you will find some of these shelters empty. Families completely wiped out, they don't have a television or radio to tell them about the danger of hiv/aids. **Just voting numbers.** *We* are on this small planet to look after each other,

Meaning helping each other,
Meaning do something to help one another,
Meaning at least try to do something to prevent other people to get into situation, we can stop by caring.
You can make a difference in your own family to prevent HIV/AIDS. Get your status and make others aware of HIV/AIDS in your town.

I can't end this book, because this is only the beginning of my story I have to tell . . . .

"HITCH HIKER"*!!!!*